glasses

eye

I ♥

MOM

skate

KAT

cake

XO

For Charlie, Gardner, Sofia, Jack, and Daniel: You've been
having adventures together since age one—
may school be the greatest one yet.

ABOUT THIS BOOK

*Every Birdie adventure has come from a piece of my own life—whether it was eagerly trying on my mom's high heels as
a little girl, fashioning outfits from unexpected places, or wishing I had a more interesting hairstyle. But this book feels
the most personal to me. As I was finishing it, my son, Charlie, was just about to start kindergarten. It was exciting,
but also scary—for BOTH of us (and Dad, too)! Charlie had questions, and I couldn't answer all of them; I could
only share my own school experiences and support him through the wonderful journey that was about to unfold.
I hope this book reminds us all that while new experiences can be scary, they can also lead to wonderful things.
I always work with watercolor and collage, but this time, I also used colored pencils, inks, and a brand of
brushes I'm not used to. I was nervous to work with new mediums, but as it turns out, I had so much fun.*

To anyone starting school or something new, congratulations! May you have the best time, always.

xo,

Sujean

*The illustrations for this book were done in watercolor, colored pencils, and collage on watercolor paper.
The text and display type were set in Horley Old Style.*

*This book was edited by Liza Baker and Allison Moore and designed by Liz Casal.
The production was supervised by Erika Schwartz, and the production editor was Wendy Dopkin.*

Copyright © 2015 by Sujean Rim • Cover art by Sujean Rim • Cover design by Liz Casal • Cover © 2015 Hachette Book Group, Inc. • All rights reserved. In accordance with the U.S. Copyright Act of 1976, the scanning, uploading, and electronic sharing of any part of this book without the permission of the publisher is unlawful piracy and theft of the author's intellectual property. If you would like to use material from the book (other than for review purposes), prior written permission must be obtained by contacting the publisher at permissions@hbgusa.com. Thank you for your support of the author's rights. • Little, Brown and Company • Hachette Book Group • 1290 Avenue of the Americas, New York, NY 10104 • Visit us at lb-kids.com • Little, Brown and Company is a division of Hachette Book Group, Inc. • The Little, Brown name and logo are trademarks of Hachette Book Group, Inc. • The publisher is not responsible for websites (or their content) that are not owned by the publisher. • First Edition: July 2015 • Library of Congress Cataloging-in-Publication Data • Rim, Sujean, author, illustrator. • Birdie's first day of school / Sujean Rim. — First edition. • pages cm • Summary: Birdie is both excited and nervous about starting school, but once she sees the classroom and meets her teacher, she knows that everything will be fine. • ISBN 978-0-316-40745-8 (hc) • [1. First day of school—Fiction. 2. Schools—Fiction.] I. Title. • PZ7.R4575Bip 2015 • [E]—dc23 • 2014014963 • 10 9 8 7 6 5 4 3 2 1 • SC

Printed in China

BIRDIE'S FIRST DAY OF SCHOOL

SUJEAN RIM

Little, Brown and Company
New York Boston

Birdie couldn't sleep.

Tomorrow would be her very first day
of school, and she was so nervous.

In the morning, Birdie asked Monster,
"What will school be like?
What should I bring?
What do I WEAR?"

Monster didn't know what to say.

While Birdie picked out just the right outfit, she wondered deep down if she was really ready for school.

She thought about all the things she'd heard.

From the good . . .

"You will learn about EVERYTHING!"

To the not-so-good . . .

"I hear it's *all work* and NO *play.*"

"I hear the *food* is *awful.*"

"I hear your *teacher*, Mr. Bobbins, is half . . . *werewolf*!"

Birdie just didn't know what to expect.

On the way to school, she sighed.
"I should be excited for my first day of school,
but I'm scared," she said to Mommy. "I wish you
and Monster could be there with me."

"Oh, sweetheart," Mommy said while putting her necklace on Birdie. "No matter where you are, no matter where you go, Monster and I are always right *here.*" Birdie hugged Mommy and felt better.

OH MY! The classroom was *beautiful.*

There was a chalkboard.

There were desks.

There were books.

There were even fish!

It had *everything*.
And everything had its place—
even Birdie!

The classroom filled up, but it was *so* quiet.

Was Mr. Bobbins really half werewolf? Birdie thought.

But as soon as he introduced himself, everyone knew he just *couldn't* be.

And soon everyone introduced themselves.
They sat in a circle, and Mr. Bobbins read
them a really great book.

Once upon a time,
a very gigantic poof

Suddenly, a magical
monkey appeared

They learned about LETTERS...

counted NUMBERS...

and even sang SONGS.

Then it was time for lunch...
and it was *delicious*.

Afterward, it was recess.

YAY! Coco, Charlie, and Eve were there!

They all played hide-and-seek with their
new friends.

Back in class, Birdie learned where some of her favorite things come from.

Did you know Italy looks just like one of Mommy's boots?

Then during art she experimented with color.

Birdie missed Mommy and Monster,
but they never felt too far away.

After school, Birdie was so excited to tell them about her day.

She told them *everything*. . . .

She felt *glad* Mr. Bobbins
was her teacher.

ciao chow

She felt *smart* from all the things she learned.

She felt *proud* of what she had done during the day.

to MOMMY

LoVE Birdie

It was time for bed...
but Birdie couldn't sleep.

Tomorrow would be her very
second day of school...
and she just couldn't wait.